# Mother Goose
# Treasury

# Mother Goose Treasury

Illustrations by
Henriette Willebeek Le Mair

FREDERICK WARNE

# Contents

Mary, Mary, Quite Contrary . . . . . . . . . . . . . . . . . . .6

Simple Simon . . . . . . . . . . . . . . . . . . . . . . . . .9

Where Are You Going To, My Pretty Maid? . . . . . .10

Sing a Song of Sixpence . . . . . . . . . . . . . . . . . . . .13

Mary Had a Little Lamb . . . . . . . . . . . . . . .14

London Bridge is Falling Down . . . . . . . . . . . . . .17

Ding, Dong, Bell . . . . . . . . . . . . . . . . . . . . . .18

Here We Go Round the Mulberry Bush . . . . . . . . .21

Three Little Kittens . . . . . . . . . . . . . . . . . . . .22

Pat-a-Cake . . . . . . . . . . . . . . . . . . . . . . . . .25

Baa, Baa, Black Sheep . . . . . . . . . . . . . . . . . . .26

Dame, Get Up and Bake Your Pies . . . . . . . . . . .29

I Love Little Pussy . . . . . . . . . . . . . . . . . . . . .30

Oh Where, Oh Where Has My Little Dog Gone? . .33

Humpty Dumpty . . . . . . . . . . . . . . . . . . . . . .34

Georgie Porgie . . . . . . . . . . . . . . . . . . . . . . . .37

Ride a Cock Horse . . . . . . . . . . . . . . . . . . . . .38

Lazy Sheep, Pray Tell Me Why? . . . . . . . . . . . . .41

Lucy Locket . . . . . . . . . . . . . . . . . . . . . . . . .42

Girls and Boys, Come Out To Play . . . . . . . . . . .45

Jack and Jill . . . . . . . . . . . . . . . . . . . . . . . . .46

Yankee Doodle . . . . . . . . . . . . . . . . . . . . . . .49

Twinkle, Twinkle, Little Star . . . . . . . . . . . . . . .50

Goosey, Goosey, Gander . . . . . . . . . . . . . . . . . .53

Oranges and Lemons . . . . . . . . . . . . . . . . . . . .54

There Was a Little Man . . . . . . . . . . . . . . . . . .57

What Are Little Boys Made Of? . . . . . . . . . . . . .58

Little Boy Blue . . . . . . . . . . . . . . . . . . . . . . .61

I Had a Little Nut Tree . . . . . . . . . . . . . . . . . .62

The Spider and the Fly . . . . . . . . . . . . . . . . . . .65

Curly Locks, Curly Locks . . . . . . . . . . . . . . . . .66

# Contents

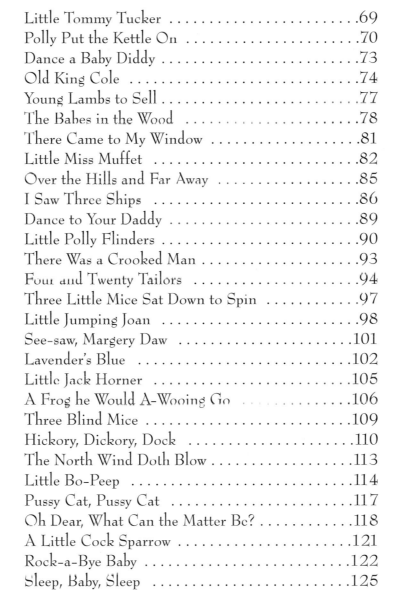

Little Tommy Tucker ........................69

Polly Put the Kettle On ....................70

Dance a Baby Diddy .......................73

Old King Cole ............................74

Young Lambs to Sell .......................77

The Babes in the Wood ....................78

There Came to My Window ................81

Little Miss Muffet ........................82

Over the Hills and Far Away ...............85

I Saw Three Ships .........................86

Dance to Your Daddy .....................89

Little Polly Flinders ......................90

There Was a Crooked Man ................93

Four and Twenty Tailors ..................94

Three Little Mice Sat Down to Spin .........97

Little Jumping Joan .......................98

See-saw, Margery Daw ...................101

Lavender's Blue ..........................102

Little Jack Horner ........................105

A Frog he Would A-Wooing Go ...........106

Three Blind Mice .........................109

Hickory, Dickory, Dock ..................110

The North Wind Doth Blow ..............113

Little Bo-Peep ...........................114

Pussy Cat, Pussy Cat .....................117

Oh Dear, What Can the Matter Be? ........118

A Little Cock Sparrow ....................121

Rock-a-Bye Baby .........................122

Sleep, Baby, Sleep ........................125


Index of First Lines ......................126

# Mary, Mary, Quite Contrary

Mary, Mary, quite contrary,
How does your garden grow?
With silver bells and cockle shells,
And pretty maids all in a row.

# Simple Simon

Simple Simon met a pieman,
　　Going to the fair;
Says Simple Simon to the pieman,
　　Let me taste your ware.

Says the pieman unto Simon,
　　Show me first your penny,
Says Simple Simon to the pieman,
　　Sir, I have not any.

Simple Simon went a-fishing,
　　For to catch a whale;
All the water he had got
　　Was in his mother's pail.

Simple Simon went to look
　　If plums grew on a thistle;
He pricked his finger very much,
　　Which made poor Simon whistle.

He went to catch a dicky bird,
　　And thought he could not fail;
Because he'd got a little salt
　　To put upon its tail.

He went for water with a sieve,
　　But soon it all fell through;
And now poor Simple Simon
　　Bids you all Adieu.

# Where Are You Going To, My Pretty Maid?

Where are you going to, my pretty maid?
    I'm going a-milking, sir, she said,
Sir, she said, sir, she said,
    I'm going a-milking, sir, she said.

May I go with you, my pretty maid?
    You're kindly welcome, sir, she said,
Sir, she said, sir, she said,
    You're kindly welcome, sir, she said.

Say, will you marry me, my pretty maid?
    Yes, if you please, kind sir, she said,
Sir, she said, sir, she said,
    Yes, if you please, kind sir, she said.

What is your father, my pretty maid?
    My father's a farmer, sir, she said,
Sir, she said, sir, she said,
    My father's a farmer, sir, she said.

What is your fortune, my pretty maid?
    My face is my fortune, sir, she said,
Sir, she said, sir, she said,
    My face is my fortune, sir, she said.

Then I can't marry you, my pretty maid.
    Nobody asked you, sir, she said,
Sir, she said, sir, she said,
    Nobody asked you, sir, she said.

# Sing a Song of Sixpence

Sing a song of sixpence,
  A pocket full of rye;
Four and twenty blackbirds,
  Baked in a pie.

When the pie was opened,
  The birds began to sing;
Was not that a dainty dish,
  To set before the king?

The king was in his counting-house,
  Counting out his money;
The queen was in the parlour,
  Eating bread and honey.

The maid was in the garden,
  Hanging out the clothes,
When down came a blackbird,
  And pecked off her nose.

# Mary Had a Little Lamb

Mary had a little lamb,
 Its fleece was white as snow;
And everywhere that Mary went —
 The lamb was sure to go.

It followed her to school one day,
 That was against the rule;
It made the children laugh and play
 To see a lamb at school.

And so the teacher turned it out,
 But still it lingered near,
And waited patiently about
 Till Mary did appear.

Why does the lamb love Mary so?
 The eager children cry;
Why, Mary loves the lamb, you know,
 The teacher did reply.

# London Bridge is Falling Down

London Bridge is falling down,
    Falling down, falling down,
London Bridge is falling down,
    My fair lady.

Build it up with wood and clay,
    Wood and clay, wood and clay,
Build it up with wood and clay,
    My fair lady.

Wood and clay will wash away,
    Wash away, wash away,
Wood and clay will wash away,
    My fair lady.

Build it up with bricks and mortar,
    Bricks and mortar, bricks and mortar,
Build it up with bricks and mortar,
    My fair lady.

Bricks and mortar will not stay,
    Will not stay, will not stay,
Bricks and mortar will not stay,
    My fair lady.

Build it up with iron and steel,
    Iron and steel, iron and steel,
Build it up with iron and steel,
    My fair lady.

Iron and steel will bend and break,
    Bend and break, bend and break,
Iron and steel will bend and break,
    My fair lady.

Build it up with silver and gold,
    Silver and gold, silver and gold,
Build it up with silver and gold,
    My fair lady.

Silver and gold will be stolen away,
    Stolen away, stolen away,
Silver and gold will be stolen away,
    My fair lady.

Set a man to watch all night,
    Watch all night, watch all night,
Set a man to watch all night,
    My fair lady.

# Ding, Dong, Bell

Ding, dong, bell,
    Pussy's in the well.
Who put her in?
    Little Johnny Green.
Who pulled her out?
    Little Tommy Stout.
What a naughty boy was that,
    To try to drown poor pussy cat,
Who never did him any harm,
    And killed the mice
    In his father's barn.

# Here We Go Round the Mulberry Bush

Here we go round the Mulberry bush,
　　The Mulberry bush, the Mulberry bush;
Here we go round the Mulberry bush
　　On a cold and frosty morning.

This is the way we wash our hands,
　　Wash our hands, wash our hands;
This is the way we wash our hands
　　On a cold and frosty morning.

This is the way we dry our hands,
　　Dry our hands, dry our hands;
This is the way we dry our hands
　　On a cold and frosty morning.

This is the way we clap our hands,
　　Clap our hands, clap our hands;
This is the way we clap our hands
　　On a cold and frosty morning.

This is the way we warm our hands,
　　Warm our hands, warm our hands;
This is the way we warm our hands
　　On a cold and frosty morning.

# Three Little Kittens

Three little kittens
They lost their mittens,
And they began to cry,
    Oh! mother dear,
    We sadly fear
    Our mittens we have lost.
What! lost your mittens,
You bad little kittens,
Then you shall have no pie.
    Mee-ow, mee-ow, mee-ow.
    Then you shall have no pie.

Three little kittens
They found their mittens,
And they began to cry,
    Oh! mother dear,
    See here, see here,
    Our mittens we have found.
What! found your mittens,
You good little kittens,
Then you shall have some pie.
    Purr, purr, purr.
    Yes, you shall have some pie.

The three little kittens
Put on their mittens,
And soon ate up the pie;
    Oh! mother dear.
    We greatly fear,
    Our mittens we have soiled.
What! soiled your mittens,
You bad little  kittens,
Then they began to sigh.
    Mee-ow, mee-ow, mee-ow.
    Then they began to sigh.

The three little kittens
They washed their mittens,
And hung them out to dry;
    Oh! mother dear,
    See here, see here,
    Our mittens we have washed.
What! washed your mittens,
You good little kittens,
But I smell a rat close by.
    Hush, hush, miew, miew,
    We smell a rat close by.

# Pat-a-Cake

Pat-a-cake, pat-a-cake, baker's man,
    Bake me a cake as fast as you can;
Pat it and prick it, and mark it with B,
    And put it in the oven for baby and me.

# Baa, Baa, Black Sheep

Baa, baa, black sheep,
Have you any wool?
Yes, sir, yes, sir,
Three bags full;
One for the master,
One for the dame,
And one for the little boy
Who lives down the lane.

# Dame, Get Up and Bake Your Pies

Dame, get up and bake your pies,
   Bake your pies, bake your pies;
Dame, get up and bake your pies,
   On Christmas day in the morning.

Dame what makes your maidens lie,
   Maidens lie, maidens lie;
Dame, what makes your maidens lie,
   On Christmas day in the morning?

Dame, what makes your ducks to die,
   Ducks to die, ducks to die;
Dame, what makes your ducks to die,
   On Christmas day in the morning?

Their wings are cut and they cannot fly,
   Cannot fly, cannot fly;
Their wings are cut and they cannot fly,
   On Christmas day in the morning.

# I Love Little Pussy

I love little pussy,
　　Her coat is so warm,
And if I don't hurt her
　　She'll do me no harm.

So I'll not pull her tail,
　　Nor drive her away,
But pussy and I
　　Together will play.

She will sit by my side
　　And I'll give her some food;
And she'll like me because
　　I'm gentle and good.

# Oh Where, Oh Where Has My Little Dog Gone?

Oh where, oh where has my little dog gone?
Oh where, oh where can he be?
With his ears cut short and his tail cut long,
Oh where, oh where is he?

# Humpty Dumpty

Humpty Dumpty sat on a wall,
    Humpty Dumpty had a great fall.
All the king's horses,
    And all the king's men,
Couldn't put Humpty together again.

# Georgie Porgie

Georgie Porgie, pudding and pie,
    Kissed the girls and made them cry;
When the boys came out to play,
    Georgie Porgie ran away.

# Ride a Cock Horse

Ride a cock horse
    To Banbury Cross,
To see a fine lady
    Upon a white horse;
With rings on her fingers
    And bells on her toes,
She shall have music
    Wherever she goes.

# Lazy Sheep, Pray Tell Me Why?

Lazy sheep, pray tell me why
    In the pleasant field you lie,
Eating grass and daisies white
    From the morning till the night?
Everything can something do,
    But what kind of use are you?

Nay, my little master, nay,
    Do not serve me so, I pray;
Don't you see the wool that grows
    On my back to make your clothes?
Cold, ah, very cold you'd be
    If you had not wool from me.

# Lucy Locket

Lucy Locket lost her pocket,
Kitty Fisher found it;
Not a penny was there in it,
Only a ribbon round it.

# Girls and Boys, Come Out To Play

Girls and boys, come out to play,
    The moon doth shine as bright as day.
Leave your supper and leave your sleep,
    And join your playfellows in the street.
Come with a whoop and come with a call,
    And come with a good will or not at all:
Up the ladder and down the wall,
    A half-penny loaf will serve us all;
You find milk, and I'll find flour,
    And we'll have a pudding in half an hour.

# Jack and Jill

Jack and Jill went up the hill
    To fetch a pail of water;
Jack fell down and broke his crown,
    And Jill came tumbling after.

Up Jack got, and home did trot,
    As fast as he could caper;
He went to bed to mend his head
    With vinegar and brown paper.

When Jill came in, how she did grin
    To see Jack's paper plaster;
Her mother vexed, she whipped her next
    For spoiling Jack's disaster.

# Yankee Doodle

Yankee doodle came to town,
    Riding on a pony;
    He stuck a feather in his cap
And called it macaroni.
    Yankee doodle, doodle do,
Yankee doodle dandy,
    All the lasses are so smart,
And sweet as sugar candy.

Marching in and marching out,
    And marching round the town, O!
Here there comes a regiment
    With Captain Thomas Brown, O!
Yankee doodle, doodle do,
    Yankee doodle dandy,
All the lasses are so smart,
    And sweet as sugar candy.

Yankee doodle is a tune
    That comes in mighty handy;
The enemy all runs away
    At Yankee doodle dandy.
Yankee doodle, doodle do,
    Yankee doodle dandy,
All the lasses are so smart,
    And sweet as sugar candy.

# Twinkle, Twinkle, Little Star

Twinkle, twinkle, little star,
    How I wonder what you are!
Up above the world so high,
    Like a diamond in the sky.

When the blazing sun is gone,
    When he nothing shines upon,
Then you show your little light,
    Twinkle, twinkle, all the night.

Then the traveller in the dark,
    Thanks you for your tiny spark,
He could not see which way to go,
    If you did not twinkle so.

In the dark blue sky you keep,
    And often through my curtains peep,
For you never shut your eye,
    Till the sun is in the sky.

As your bright and tiny spark,
    Lights the traveller in the dark,
Though I know not what you are,
    Twinkle, twinkle, little star.

# Goosey, Goosey, Gander

Goosey, goosey, gander
    Whither shall I wander?
Upstairs and downstairs
    And in my lady's chamber.
There I met an old man
    Who would not say his prayers.
I took him by the left leg
    And threw him down the stairs.

# Oranges and Lemons

Oranges and lemons,
Say the bells of St. Clement's.

You owe me five farthings,
Say the bells of St. Martin's.

When will you pay me?
Say the bells of Old Bailey.

When I grow rich,
Say the bells of Shoreditch.

When will that be?
Say the bells of Stepney.

I do not know,
Says the great bell of Bow.

Here comes a candle
To light you to bed.

Here comes a chopper
To chop off your head!

# There Was a Little Man

There was a little man,
  And he wooed a little maid,
And he said, Little maid,
  Will you wed, wed, wed?
  I have little more to say,
  Than will you, yea or nay?
For the least said is soonest
    mended, ded, ded.

The little maid replied,
  If I should be your bride,
Pray what must we have
    For to eat, eat, eat?
    Will the love that you're so rich in
    Make a fire in the kitchen,
And the little god of love
    turn the spit, spit, spit?

Then the little man he sighed,
  Some say a little cried,
And his little heart was big
    With sorrow, sorrow, sorrow;
    I'll be your little slave,
    And if the little that I have
Be too little, little dear,
    I will borrow, borrow, borrow.

Thus did the little gent
  Make the little maid relent,
For her little heart began
    To beat, beat, beat;
    Though his offers were but small,
    She accepted of them all,
Now she thanks her little stars
    for her fate, fate, fate.

# What Are Little Boys Made Of?

What are little boys made of?
　　What are little boys made of?
Frogs and snails and puppy-dogs' tails,
　　That's what little boys are made of.

What are little girls made of?
　　What are little girls made of?
Sugar and spice and all that's nice,
　　That's what little girls are made of.

# Little Boy Blue

Little Boy Blue,
  Come blow your horn,
The sheep's in the meadow,
  The cow's in the corn;
Where's the boy
  Who looks after the sheep?
He's under a haystack
  Fast asleep.
Will you wake him?
  No, not I!
  For if I do, he's sure to cry.

# I Had a Little Nut Tree

I had a little nut tree,
    Nothing would it bear
But a silver nutmeg
    And a golden pear;
The King of Spain's daughter
    Came to visit me;
And all for the sake
    Of my little nut tree.

# The Spider and the Fly

Will you walk into my parlour?
Said the spider to the fly.
 'Tis the prettiest little parlour
 That you ever did espy;
The way into my parlour
Is up a winding stair,
 And I have many pretty things
 To show you when you're there.
Oh, no, no! said the little fly,
To ask me is in vain,
 For who goes up your winding stair
 Shall ne'er come down again.

The spider turned him round about
And went into his den,
 For well he knew the silly fly
 Would soon come back again;
So he wove a subtle web
In a little corner sly,
 And he set his table ready,
 To dine upon the fly:
Then he came out to his door again
And merrily did sing,
 Come hither, hither, pretty fly,
 With the pearl and silver wing.

Alas! alas! how very soon
This silly little fly,
 Hearing all these flattering speeches
 Came quickly buzzing by;
With gauzy wing she hung aloft,
Then near and nearer drew,
 Thinking only of her crested head
 And gold and purple hue,
Thinking only of her brilliant wings
Poor silly thing, at last
 Up jumped the wicked spider
 And fiercely held her fast.

# Curly Locks, Curly Locks

Curly locks, Curly locks,
    Wilt thou be mine?
Thou shalt not wash dishes
    Nor yet feed the swine;
But sit on a cushion
    And sew a fine seam,
And feed upon strawberries,
    Sugar and cream.

# Little Tommy Tucker

Little Tommy Tucker
  Sings for his supper:
What shall we give him?
  White bread and butter.
How shall he cut it
  Without a knife?
How will he be married
  Without a wife?

# Polly Put the Kettle On

Polly put the kettle on,
Polly put the kettle on,
Polly put the kettle on,
   We'll all have tea.

Sukey take it off again,
Sukey take it off again,
Sukey take it off again,
   They've all gone away.

# Dance a Baby Diddy

Dance a baby diddy,
    What can mammy do wid 'e
But sit in her lap,
    And give 'un some pap
And dance a baby diddy?

# Old King Cole

Old King Cole
    Was a merry old soul,
And a merry old soul was he;
    He called for his pipe,
And he called for his bowl,
And he called for his fiddlers three.

Every fiddler
    Had a fine fiddle,
And a very fine fiddle had he;
    Oh there's none so rare
As can compare
With King Cole and his fiddlers three.

# Young Lambs to Sell

Young lambs to sell!
    Young lambs to sell!
I never would cry
    Young lambs to sell,
If I'd as much money
    As I could tell
I never would cry
    Young lambs to sell.

# The Babes in the Wood

My dears, you must know,
That a long time ago,
　　Two poor little children
　　Whose names I don't know,
Were stolen away
On a fine summer's day,
　　And left in a wood,
　　As I've heard the folk say.
Poor Babes in the Wood!
Poor Babes in the Wood!
　　Don't you remember
　　The Babes in the Wood?

And when it was night,
So sad was their plight,
　　The sun it went down,
　　And the moon gave no light;
They sobb'd and they sigh'd
And they bitterly cried,
　　And the poor little things
　　They then lay down and died.
Poor Babes in the Wood!
Poor Babes in the Wood!
　　Don't you remember
　　The Babes in the Wood?

And when they were dead,
The robins so red,
　　Brought strawberry leaves
　　To over them spread,
Then all the day long
The branches among,
　　They mournfully whistled,
　　And this was their song:
Poor Babes in the Wood!
Poor Babes in the Wood!
　　Don't you remember
　　The Babes in the Wood?

# There Came to My Window

There came to my window
    One morning in spring
A sweet little robin,
    She came there to sing;
The tune that she sang
    It was prettier far
Then any I heard
    On the flute or guitar.

Her wings she was spreading
    To soar far away,
Then resting a moment
    Seem'd sweetly to say –
Oh happy, how happy
    The world seems to be,
Awake, little girl,
    And be happy with me!

# Little Miss Muffet

Little Miss Muffet
      Sat on a tuffet,
Eating her curds and whey;
      There came a big spider,
Who sat down beside her
      And frightened Miss Muffet away.

# Over the Hills and Far Away

Tom, he was a piper's son,
    He learnt to play when he was young,
And all the tune that he could play,
    Was, 'Over the hills and far away';
Over the hills and a great way off,
    The wind shall blow my top-knot off.

Tom with his pipe made such a noise,
    That he pleased both the girls and boys,
And they all stopped to hear him play,
    'Over the hills and far away'.
Over the hills and a great way off,
    The wind shall blow my top-knot off.

# I Saw Three Ships

I saw three ships come sailing by,
    Come sailing by, come sailing by,
I saw three ships come sailing by,
    On New-Year's day in the morning.

And what do you think was in them then,
    Was in them then, was in them then?
And what do you think was in them then,
    On New-Year's day in the morning.

Three pretty girls were in them then,
    Were in them then, were in them then,
Three pretty girls were in them then,
    On New-Year's day in the morning.

One could whistle, and one could sing,
    And one could play on the violin;
Such joy there was at my wedding,
    On New-Year's day in the morning.

# Dance to Your Daddy

Dance to your daddy,
My little babby,
Dance to your daddy,
My little lamb!

You shall have a fishy
In a little dishy,
You shall have a fishy
When the boat comes in!

# Little Polly Flinders

Little Polly Flinders
    Sat among the cinders,
Warming her pretty little toes;
    Her mother came and caught her,
And whipped her little daughter
For spoiling her nice new clothes.

# There Was a Crooked Man

There was a crooked man,
    And he walked a crooked mile,
He found a crooked sixpence
    Upon a crooked stile;
He bought a crooked cat,
    Which caught a crooked mouse,
And they all lived together
    In a little crooked house.

# Four and Twenty Tailors

Four and twenty tailors
    Went to catch a snail,
The best man among them
    Durst not touch her tail;
She put out her horns
    Like a little Kyloe cow,
Run, tailors, run,
    Or she'll kill you all e'en now.

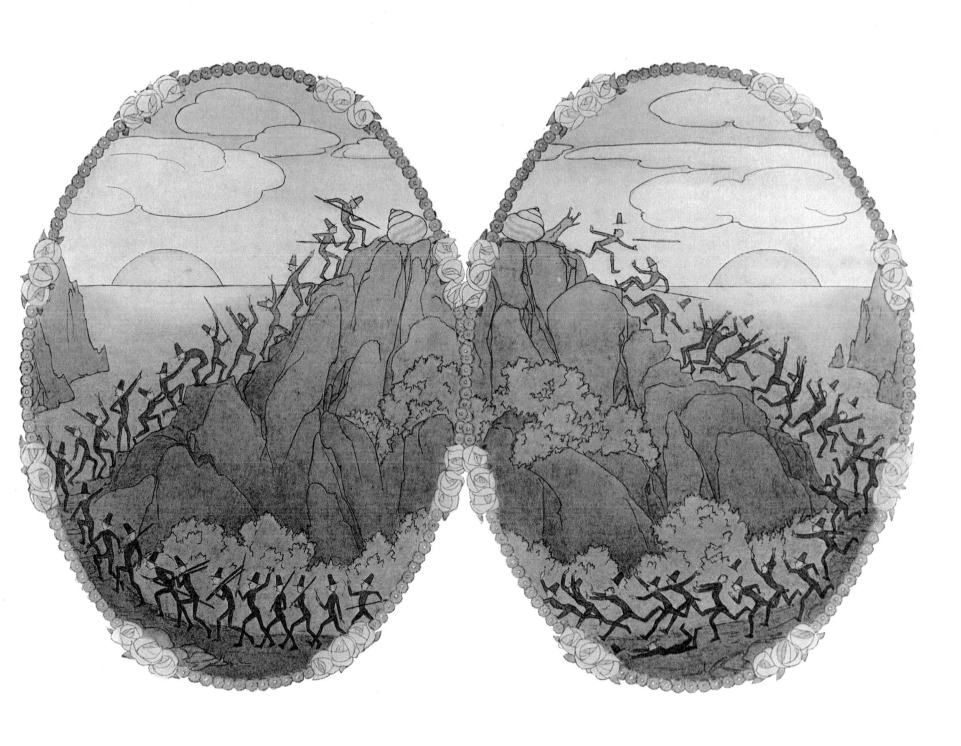

# Three Little Mice Sat Down to Spin

Three little mice sat down to spin;
    Pussy passed by and she peeped in.
What are you doing, my little men?
    Weaving coats for Gentlemen.
Shall I come in and cut off your threads?
    No, no, Mistress Pussy, you'd bite off our heads.
Oh, no, I'll not; I'll help you spin.
    That may be so, but you don't come in.

# Little Jumping Joan

Here am I,
          Little Jumping Joan;
When nobody's with me
          I'm all alone.

# See-saw, Margery Daw

See-saw, Margery Daw,
  Johnny shall have a new master;
He shall have but a penny a day,
  Because he can't work any faster.

# Lavender's Blue

Lavender's blue, dilly, dilly,
Lavender's green;
When I am king, dilly, dilly,
You shall be queen.

Call up your men, dilly, dilly,
Set them to work,
Some to the plough, dilly, dilly,
Some to the cart.

Some to make hay, dilly, dilly,
Some to thresh corn,
While you and I, dilly, dilly,
Keep ourselves warm.

# Little Jack Horner

Little Jack Horner
    Sat in a corner,
Eating his Christmas pie;
    He put in his thumb,
    And pulled out a plum,
And said 'What a good boy am I!'

# A Frog He Would A-Wooing Go

A frog he would a-wooing go,
　　Heigh-ho! says Rowley;
Whether his mother
Would let him or no,
　　With a rowley, powley,
　　Gammon and spinach,
Heigh-ho! says Anthony Rowley.

So off he set with his opera hat,
　　Heigh-ho! says Rowley;
And on the road
He met with a rat,
　　With a rowley, powley, etc.

Pray, Mister Rat, will you go with me?
　　Heigh-ho! says Rowley;
Kind Mistress Mousey
For to see,
　　With a rowley, powley, etc.

They came to the door of Mousey's Hall,
　　Heigh-ho! says Rowley;
They gave a loud knock,
And they gave a loud call,
　　With a rowley, powley, etc.

Pray, Missy Mouse, are you within?
　　Heigh-ho! says Rowley;
Oh yes, kind sirs,
I'm sitting to spin,
　　With a rowley, powley, etc.

Pray, Missy Mouse, do give us some beer,
　　Heigh-ho! says Rowley;
For Froggy and I
Are fond of good cheer,
　　With a rowley, powley, etc.

Pray, Mister Frog, please give us a song?
　　Heigh-ho! says Rowley;
Let it be something
That's not over long,
　　With a rowley, powley, etc.

But while all were a-merry-making,
　　Heigh-ho! says Rowley;
A cat and her kittens
Came tumbling in,
　　With a rowley, powley, etc.

The cat she seized the rat by the crown,
　　Heigh-ho! says Rowley;
The kittens they pulled
The little mouse down,
　　With a rowley, powley, etc.

This put Mister Frog in a terrible fright,
　　Heigh-ho! says Rowley;
He took up his hat and
He wished them good-night,
　　With a rowley, powley, etc.

But as Froggy was crossing over a brook,
　　Heigh-ho! says Rowley;
A lily-white duck came
And gobbled him up,
　　With a rowley, powley, etc.

So there was the end of one, two & three.
　　Heigh-ho! says Rowley;
The rat, the mouse,
And the little froggy,
　　With a rowley, powley,
　　Gammon and spinach,
Heigh-ho! says Anthony Rowley.

# Three Blind Mice

Three blind mice, see how they run!
They all run after the farmer's wife,
　　Who cut off their tails with a carving knife,
Did ever you see such a thing in your life,
　　As three blind mice?

# Hickory, Dickory, Dock

Hickory, dickory, dock,
    The mouse ran up the clock;
The clock struck one,
    The mouse ran down,
Hickory, dickory, dock.

Hickory, dickory, dare,
    The pig flew up in the air;
The man in brown
    Soon brought him down,
Hickory, dickory, dare.

# The North Wind Doth Blow

The north wind doth blow,
　　And we shall have snow,
And what will poor robin do then,
　　Poor thing?
He'll sit in a barn,
　　And keep himself warm,
And hide his head under his wing,
　　Poor thing.

# Little Bo-Peep

Little Bo-Peep has lost her sheep,
And doesn't know where to find them;
    Leave them alone,
    And they'll come home,
Bringing their tails behind them.

Little Bo-Peep fell fast asleep,
And dreamt she heard them bleating;
    But when she awoke,
    She found it a joke,
For they were still a-fleeting.

Then up she took her little crook,
Determined for to find them;
    She found them indeed,
    But it made her heart bleed,
For they'd left their tails behind them.

It happened one day, as Bo-Peep did stray
Into a meadow hard by,
    There she espied
    Their tails side by side,
All hung on a tree to dry.

She heaved a sigh, and wiped her eye,
And went over hill and dale, O!
    And tried what she could
    As a shepherdess should
To tack to each sheep its tail, O!

# Pussy Cat, Pussy Cat

Pussy cat, pussy cat,
　Where have you been?
I've been to London
　　To look at the queen.
Pussy cat, pussy cat,
　What did you there?
I frightened a little mouse
　　Under her chair.

# Oh Dear, What Can the Matter Be?

Oh dear, what can the matter be?
　　Dear, dear, what can the matter be?
Oh dear, what can the matter be?
　　Johnny's so long at the fair.

He promised he'd bring me a basket of posies,
　　A garland of lilies, a garland of roses,
He promised to bring me a bunch of blue ribbons
　　To tie up my bonny brown hair.

# A Little Cock Sparrow

A little cock sparrow
Sat on a green tree,
    And he chirruped, he chirruped,
    So merry was he.
A naughty boy came
With his wee bow and arrow,
    Says he, I will shoot
    This little cock sparrow;
His body will make me
A nice little stew,
    And his giblets will make me
    A little pie too.
Oh, no, said the sparrow,
I won't make a stew,
    So he flapped his wings
    And away he flew.

# Rock-a-Bye Baby

Rock-a-bye baby,
  On the tree top.
When the wind blows
  The cradle will rock;
When the bough breaks
  The cradle will fall.
Down will come baby,
  Cradle and all.

# Sleep, Baby, Sleep

Sleep, baby, sleep!
    Our cottage vale is deep;
The little lamb is on the green,
    With woolly fleece so soft and clean.
Sleep, baby, sleep!

Sleep, baby, sleep!
    Thy rest shall angels keep,
While on the grass the lamb shall feed,
    And never suffer want or need.
Sleep, baby, sleep!

Sleep, baby, sleep!
    Down where the woodbines creep;
Be always like the lamb so mild,
    A kind, and sweet, and gentle child.
Sleep, baby, sleep!

# Index of First Lines

A little cock sparrow . . . . . . . . . . . . . . . . . . . . . . . . . . . . . . . .121

Baa, baa, black sheep, . . . . . . . . . . . . . . . . . . . . . . . . . . . . . . .26

Curly locks, Curly locks, . . . . . . . . . . . . . . . . . . . . . . . . . . . . .66

Dame, get up and bake your pies, . . . . . . . . . . . . . . . . . . . .29

Dance a baby diddy, . . . . . . . . . . . . . . . . . . . . . . . . . . . . . . . .73

Dance to your daddy, . . . . . . . . . . . . . . . . . . . . . . . . . . . . . . .89

Ding, dong, bell, . . . . . . . . . . . . . . . . . . . . . . . . . . . . . . . . . . .18

Four and twenty tailors . . . . . . . . . . . . . . . . . . . . . . . . . . . . .94

A frog he would a-wooing go, . . . . . . . . . . . . . . . . . . . . . . .106

Georgie Porgie, pudding and pie, . . . . . . . . . . . . . . . . . . . .37

Girls and boys come out to play, . . . . . . . . . . . . . . . . . . . . .45

Goosey, goosey, gander . . . . . . . . . . . . . . . . . . . . . . . . . . . . .53

Here am I, . . . . . . . . . . . . . . . . . . . . . . . . . . . . . . . . . . . . . . . .98

Here we go round the Mulberry bush, . . . . . . . . . . . . . . . .21

Hickory, dickory, dock, . . . . . . . . . . . . . . . . . . . . . . . . . . . .110

Humpty Dumpty sat on a wall, . . . . . . . . . . . . . . . . . . . . . .34

I had a little nut tree, . . . . . . . . . . . . . . . . . . . . . . . . . . . . . .62

I love little pussy, . . . . . . . . . . . . . . . . . . . . . . . . . . . . . . . . . .30

I saw three ships come sailing by, . . . . . . . . . . . . . . . . . . . .86

Jack and Jill went up the hill . . . . . . . . . . . . . . . . . . . . . . . .46

Lavender's blue, dilly, dilly, . . . . . . . . . . . . . . . . . . . . . . . . .102

Lazy sheep, pray tell me why . . . . . . . . . . . . . . . . . . . . . . . .41

Little Bo-Peep has lost her sheep, . . . . . . . . . . . . . . . . . . .114

Little Boy Blue, . . . . . . . . . . . . . . . . . . . . . . . . . . . . . . . . . . .61

Little Jack Horner . . . . . . . . . . . . . . . . . . . . . . . . . . . . . . . .105

Little Miss Muffet . . . . . . . . . . . . . . . . . . . . . . . . . . . . . . . . .82

Little Polly Flinders . . . . . . . . . . . . . . . . . . . . . . . . . . . . . . .90

Little Tommy Tucker . . . . . . . . . . . . . . . . . . . . . . . . . . . . . .69

London Bridge is falling down, . . . . . . . . . . . . . . . . . . . . . . . . . . . . . .17

Lucy Locket lost her pocket, . . . . . . . . . . . . . . . . . . . . . . . . . . . . . .42

Mary had a little lamb, . . . . . . . . . . . . . . . . . . . . . . . . . . . . . .14

Mary, Mary, quite contrary, . . . . . . . . . . . . . . . . . . . . . . . . . . . .6

My dears, you must know, . . . . . . . . . . . . . . . . . . . . . . . . . . . . . .78

Oh dear, what can the matter be? . . . . . . . . . . . . . . . . . . . . . . . .118

Oh where, oh where has my little dog gone? . . . . . . . . . . . . . . . .33

Old King Cole . . . . . . . . . . . . . . . . . . . . . . . . . . . . . . . . . . . . .74

Oranges and lemons, . . . . . . . . . . . . . . . . . . . . . . . . . . . . . .54

Pat-a-cake, pat-a-cake, baker's man, . . . . . . . . . . . . . . . . . . . . .25

Polly put the kettle on, . . . . . . . . . . . . . . . . . . . . . . . . . . . . . .70

Pussy cat, pussy cat, . . . . . . . . . . . . . . . . . . . . . . . . . . . . . . .117

Ride a cock horse . . . . . . . . . . . . . . . . . . . . . . . . . . . . . . . . . .38

Rock-a-bye baby . . . . . . . . . . . . . . . . . . . . . . . . . . . . . . . . . .122

See-saw, Margery Daw, . . . . . . . . . . . . . . . . . . . . . . . . . . . . .101

Sing a song of sixpence, . . . . . . . . . . . . . . . . . . . . . . . . . . . . .13

Simple Simon met a pieman, . . . . . . . . . . . . . . . . . . . . . . . . . .9

Sleep, baby, sleep! . . . . . . . . . . . . . . . . . . . . . . . . . . . . . . . . .125

The north wind doth blow, . . . . . . . . . . . . . . . . . . . . . . . . . .113

There came to my window . . . . . . . . . . . . . . . . . . . . . . . . . . .81

There was a crooked man, . . . . . . . . . . . . . . . . . . . . . . . . . . . .93

There was a little man, . . . . . . . . . . . . . . . . . . . . . . . . . . . . . .57

Three blind mice, see how they run! . . . . . . . . . . . . . . . . . . . .109

Three little kittens . . . . . . . . . . . . . . . . . . . . . . . . . . . . . . . . .22

Three little mice sat down to spin; . . . . . . . . . . . . . . . . . . . . . .97

Tom, he was a piper's son, . . . . . . . . . . . . . . . . . . . . . . . . . . .85

Twinkle, twinkle, little star, . . . . . . . . . . . . . . . . . . . . . . . . . .50

What are little boys made of? . . . . . . . . . . . . . . . . . . . . . . . . .58

Where are you going to, my pretty maid? . . . . . . . . . . . . . . . . .10

Will you walk into my parlour? . . . . . . . . . . . . . . . . . . . . . . . .65

Yankee doodle came to town, . . . . . . . . . . . . . . . . . . . . . . . . .49

Young lambs to sell! . . . . . . . . . . . . . . . . . . . . . . . . . . . . . . . .77

FREDERICK WARNE
Published by the Penguin Group
Penguin Books Ltd, 27 Wrights Lane, London W8 5TZ, England
Penguin Putnam Inc., 375 Hudson Street, New York, NY 10014, USA
Penguin Books Australia Ltd, Ringwood, Victoria, Australia
Penguin Books Canada Ltd, 10 Alcorn Avenue, Toronto, Ontario, Canada M4V 3B2
Penguin Books (NZ) Ltd, Private Bag 102902, NSMC, Auckland, New Zealand

Penguin Books Ltd, Registered Offices: Harmondsworth, Middlesex, England

Originally published by Augener Ltd in two separate volumes:
*Our Old Nursery Rhymes* and *Little Songs of Long Ago*, 1911 and 1912
First published in this format 1999 by Frederick Warne

1 3 5 7 9 10 8 6 4 2

Illustrations copyright © Soefi Stichting Inayat Fundatie Sirdar, 1999
This presentation copyright © Frederick Warne & Co., 1999

ISBN 0 7232 4549 5

Printed and bound in Singapore by Tien Wah Press (Pte) Ltd
Colour reproduction by Anglia Graphics, Bedford, England